If I Lived Alone

by Michaela Muntean

Illustrated by Carol Nicklaus

Featuring Jim Henson's
Sesame Street Muppets

A SESAME STREET/GOLDEN PRESS BOOK
Published by Western Publishing Company, Inc.
in conjunction with Children's Television Workshop.

©1980 Children's Television Workshop.
Muppet characters ©1980 Muppets, Inc. All rights reserved. Printed in U.S.A.
SESAME STREET®, the SESAME STREET SIGN, and SESAME STREET BOOK CLUB
are trademarks and service marks of Children's Television Workshop.
GOLDEN® and GOLDEN PRESS® are trademarks of Western Publishing Company, Inc.
No part of this book may be reproduced or copied in any form without
written permission from the publisher.
Library of Congress Catalog Card Number: 80-51205
ISBN 0-307-23118-6

This is where I live.

My Mommy and Daddy live here.
My big sister Frieda and little brother Roger live here.

Sometimes it's noisy in my house.

Sometimes it's crowded in my house.

Sometimes I have to be quiet because Roger is asleep.

Sometimes I wish I lived alone.

If I lived alone, I could have a room all to myself and everything in it would be MINE! I could sit quietly all by myself, or I could make as much noise as I wanted whenever I wanted to.

But if I lived alone, I wouldn't have anyone to
talk to when it rains and thunders.

If I lived alone, I could eat chocolate ice cream for breakfast, vanilla ice cream for lunch, and strawberry ice cream for dinner. And I could eat as much as I wanted.

But if I lived alone, I wouldn't get to have any of Daddy's super-duper, flip-flop flapjacks.

If I lived alone, I wouldn't have to share my toys and books.

But if I lived alone, who would read to me?

If I lived alone, I could stay up as late as I wanted to.

But if I lived alone, who would hug me and kiss me and tuck me in bed?

If I lived alone, I wouldn't have to help set the table,
or pick up my toys, or do anything I didn't want to do.

But if I lived alone, who would help me tie my shoelaces and who would put a bandage on my knee if I fell down?

If I lived alone, who would play baseball with Daddy?

Who would help him weed the garden?

If I lived alone, who would help Mommy with her sculpture?

Who would talk to her when she takes Roger for a walk?

If I lived alone, who would listen to Frieda's secrets?

Who would share Roger's crackers?

I guess I can't live alone—because if I lived alone,
everyone would be lonely.

ABCDEFGH